PHOENIX YARD
BOOKS

Hot Air

Sandrine Dumas Roy   Emmanuelle Houssais

Sarah Ardizzone

The **ice** had melted even faster than usual.

The **wolf** got stuck on a tiny island drifting mid-ocean.

The **reindeer** nearly drowned trying to reach her summer home.

And the **polar bear** needed a new outfit because the landscape wasn't as white.

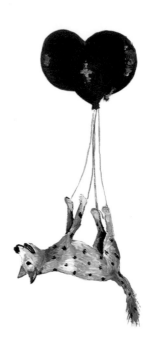

Animals in other parts of the
world were struggling too.

The dingo went **doolally**
after his fur turned brown
and spotty.

Even the gecko was too hot to sunbathe comfortably.

And the kangaroo had to jump further each day because there wasn't enough grass.

The same complaint rose up from every corner of the planet.

"The sun is too hot and there's no getting away from it. We're gasping for air and there's not enough rain."

So the animals decided to hold a conference with the title:

Coo n cofn

"What's wrong with the weather?"

What a racket!

There was **shouting** and babbling.
Cackling, **clattering** and chatterering.
Giggling, gurgling and **gobbling**.
Cheeping, chirping and **yelping**.
Screeching, **hissing** and humming.
Hooting, cooing and **crooning**.

"If we want to find a **solution**, we need to get to the **bottom** of the **problem**."
That was the only thing everyone agreed on.

Dolphins were dispatched around the world on a fact-finding mission.

From the Yellow River to the Amazon,
the Arctic Ocean to the Pacific,
the Strait of Gibraltar to the Madagascar Strait
the Gulf of Alaska to the Gulf of Aqaba,
and the Tasman Sea to the Sea of Oman,
they trawled for evidence.

Once the results were in, there was no escaping the truth.

The planet was heating up,
that much **was clear.**
But why?

Cows!

Un-be-lievable. But true.
"There are gazillions of them.
And they spend their days grazing,
ruminating, farting
and burping."

"Their gassy
emissions are
making the wind go

haywire

and the seasons go

topsy-turvy."

When the animals met up again
the debate was **red-hot**.

Some suggested a **complete ban** on all cows.
But the carnivores were outraged
(their roast beef was at stake!).

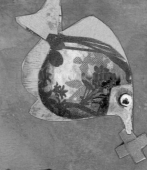

"What if the cows were only
allowed to eat every other day?"

"Hmm... that might reduce gas levels,
    but it wouldn't solve the problem completely."

    The surgeonfish offered to remove
        two or three of the cows' four stomachs.

"If they eat less, they'll fart less!"

"How about a **change of diet?**"

suggested the flamingo.

"The cows could eat GM foods low in gases (Gas Moderate) to reduce air pollution."

"Or we could try genetically modifying them: dwarf cows are bound to produce teeny-weeny **farts.**"

But none of these ideas
seemed like the right answer.

"Oh, holy cow!
They get VIP status
in some places."

"Just try persuading
burger-eaters to
change their ways."

"Those rodeo-riding cowboys
and their bucking broncos
will go out of business."

The animals were in a tizzy.

"If the cows don't stop grazing, it's only a matter of time before we all become extinct."

"By tinkering with our tubes, we could produce fizzy milk instead of farts," suggested the cows, who felt guilty about their gas and wanted to put a cork in it.

But the **bubbles** in the milk would still be released **back into the atmosphere...**

Then a porpoise had
a preposterous idea.

"The cows must go full steam ahead
with maximum fart-production!"

Flummoxed, the other animals made fun of her:

"Poor porpoise, she's lost the plot!"

But the porpoise explained
her thinking:

"We need to collect all the
farts produced by the cows,
and use their gas
to power a giant
factory that will
freeze the ice."

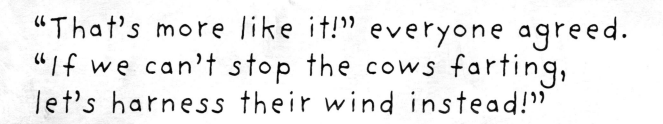

"That's more like it!" everyone agreed.
"If we can't stop the cows farting,
let's harness their wind instead!"

Thunderous applause.

The delegates left the meeting **fizzing** and **popping**.

They just had to persuade the cows to be fitted with cowtalytic converters (the most efficient way of converting farts).

After long negotiations, the cows gave their consent. But it took years to build the factory and get it up and running.

The big day came at last. Bigwigs patted each other on the back when the factory opened:

"Didn't we find a tip-top solution?"

Except that most of the ice had already melted.

Recently, there's been even
more flooding than usual ...

Hot Air

ISBN: 978-1-907912-22-1

First published in French in 2009 under the title
Chaude la Planète by Les Editions du Ricochet.

This edition published in Great Britain
by Phoenix Yard Books Ltd, 2013.

Phoenix Yard Books
Phoenix Yard
65 King's Cross Road
London
WC1X 9LW

1 3 5 7 9 10 8 6 4 2

A CIP catalogue record for this book is available from the British Library

Printed in China

www.phoenixyardbooks.com